4   5 billion years ago, our planet, Earth, forms.

3   1 billion years after the Big Bang, the galaxies begin to take shape.

8   2.5 billion years ago, our breathable atmosphere forms.

7   3 billion years ago, life begins with the appearance of the first bacteria and blue algae.

Tyrannosaurus

Vol. 6

Argentinosaurus

Baryonyx

Triceratops

Vol. 5

Camarasaurus

Vol. 4

Cretaceous

Scipionyx

Giganotosaurus

CONTENTS

First published in the United States of America in 2009 by Abbeville
Press, 137 Varick Street, New York, NY 10013

First published in Italy in 2009 by Editoriale Jaca Book S.p.A.,
via Frua 11, 20146 Milano

First edition
10 9 8 7 6 5 4 3 2 1

Library of Congress Cataloging-in-Publication Data

Bacchin, Matteo.
  The hunting pack : Allosaurus / Matteo Bacchin
    p. cm.
  ISBN 978-0-7892-1011-1 (alk. paper)
  1. Allosaurus--Juvenile literature. I. Title.
  QE862.S3B328 2010
  567.912--dc22
                    2009016834

For bulk and premium sales and for text adoption procedures, write
to Customer Service Manager, Abbeville Press, 137 Varick Street,
New York, NY 10013, or call 1-800-ARTBOOK.

Visit Abbeville Press online at www.abbeville.com.

For the English-language edition: Austin Allen, editor;
Ashley Benning, copy editor; Louise Kurtz, production manager;
Robert Weisberg, composition; Ada Blazer, cover design.

Foreword
By Mark Norell

In the mid-nineteenth century, not much was known of dinosaurs. A few fossil fragments had been found in the English countryside, and a remarkable series of ancient plant-eaters had been excavated from a Belgian coal mine. These scant remains gave contemporary paleontologists their first early conceptions of what dinosaurs looked like. Yet while larger than any living reptiles, these animals were not particularly huge; they do not capture the imagination as dinosaurs in today's museums, movies, and TV shows do.

The discovery of dinosaur bones in America near Morrison, Colorado in the 1860s would quickly rock the scientific world. Bones in this area are so common that one famous locality was marked by a shepherd's cabin constructed of dinosaur fossils. Here lived a tremendous diversity of dinosaurs, including giants like *Diplodocus*, *Apatosaurus*, and *Camarasaurus*; weird spiked animals like *Stegosaurus*; and fearsome predators like *Allosaurus*. These were (and still are) some of the largest animals ever to walk the planet, and there was much contemporary speculation about their habits and capabilities. These are also the animals that greet visitors in the exhibition halls of today's great museums.

Our knowledge of the Morrison Formation has changed drastically in the ensuing years as excavations have been carried out more systematically and careful attention paid to the characteristics of the surrounding rocks. We now believe that during Morrison times there was a vast floodplain existing along a shallow sea in what is today the mid-continent mountainous belt of North America. This floodplain was more arid in the south and was bisected by flowing rivers and streams. It was a rich area, teeming with aquatic and terrestrial plants and animals.

Some of the remarkable areas that have been excavated, including those described in this book, seem to pose as many questions as they answer. For instance, the Cleveland-Lloyd Quarry in Utah preserves the skeletons of literally hundreds of specimens of the carnivore *Allosaurus*. Is this evidence of a pack that was catastrophically wiped out, or of a cluster of skeletons that simply accumulated through the years, or even of a death pit where *Allosauruses* were trapped by quicksand or sticky mud? The Morrison record is good—but still not quite good enough to help us pinpoint the true scenario among these intriguing alternatives.

DINOSAURS

THE HUNTING PACK
ALLOSAURUS

DINOSAURS

The Hunting Pack

ALLOSAURUS

Drawings and story
MATTEO BACCHIN

Essays and story
MARCO SIGNORE

Translated from the Italian
by Marguerite Shore

ABBEVILLE KIDS
A Division of Abbeville Publishing Group
New York London

5

3

6

2

5

4

3

2

4

5

7

8

9

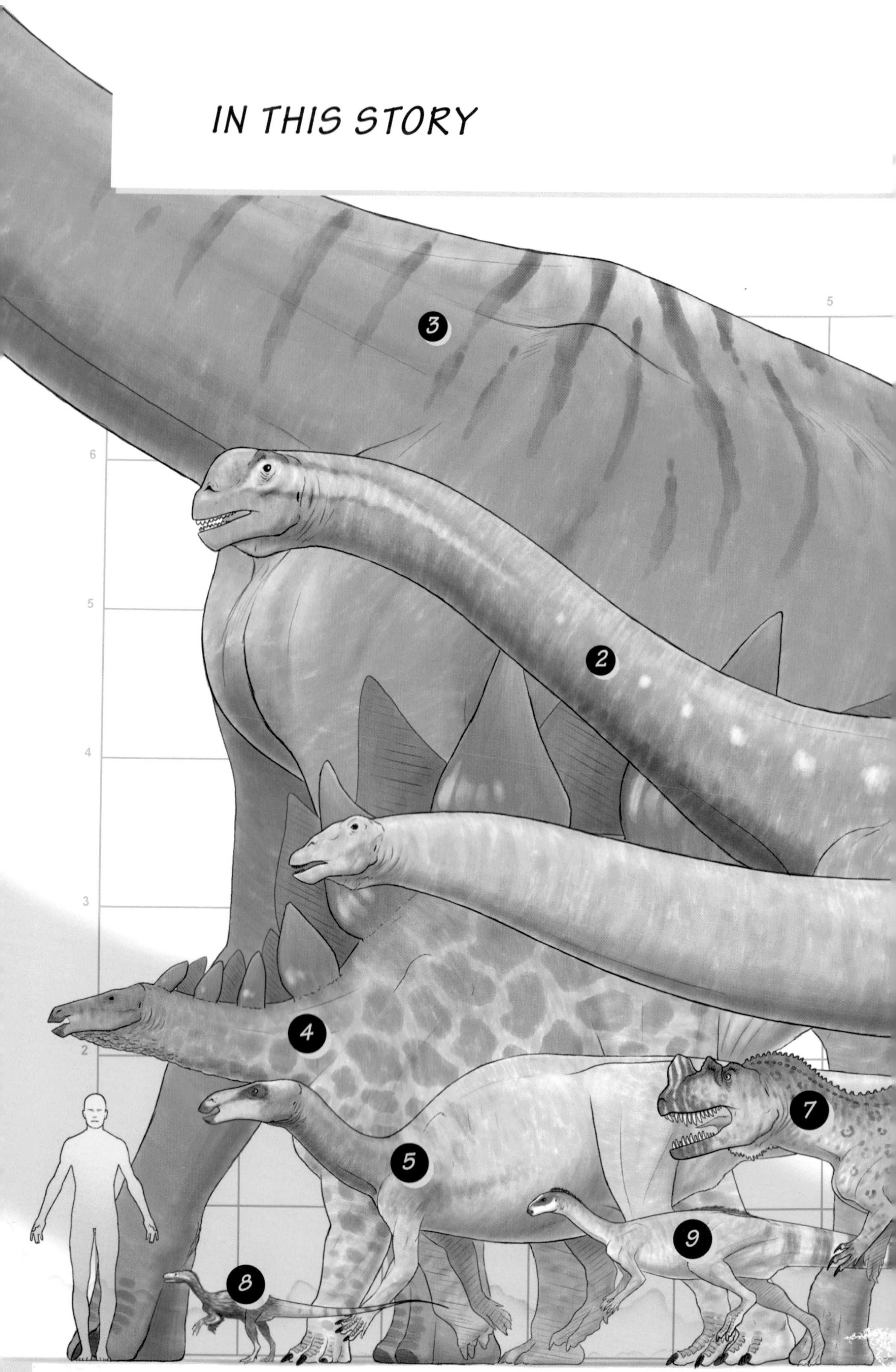

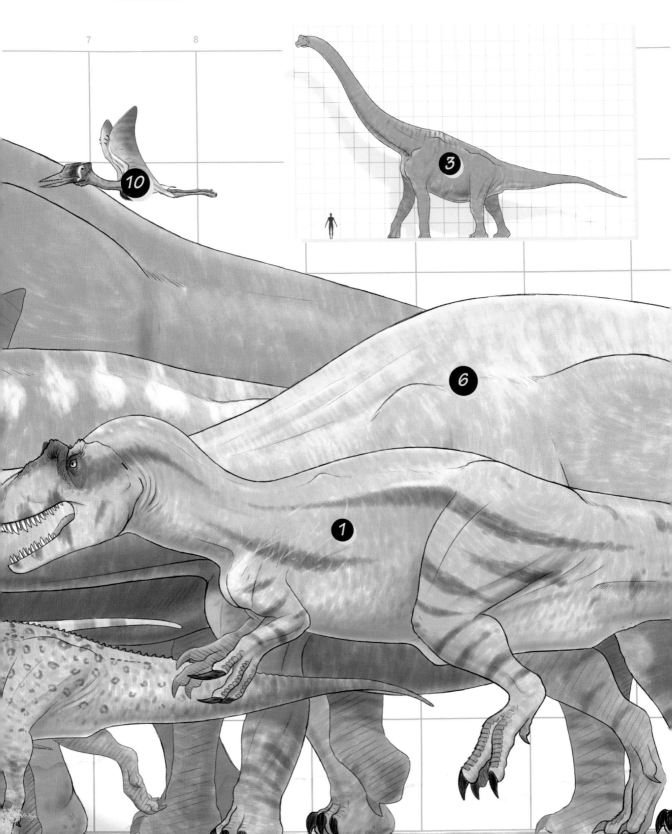

1. Allosaurus
2. Camarasaurus
3. Brachiosaurus
4. Stegosaurus
5. Camptosaurus
6. Apatosaurus
7. Ceratosaurus
8. Ornitholestes
9. Ornitholestes
10. Pterosaur

See identikit on page 40

THE NARRATOR

ALLOW ME TO INTRODUCE MYSELF ONCE AGAIN:
I AM A SUN. A YELLOW SUN.
AS YOU ALREADY KNOW, I AM NOT THE BRIGHTEST
OR THE MOST POWERFUL, NOR EVEN THE FIRSTBORN SON OF
THE INFINITE MOTHER UNIVERSE.
IN FACT, I AM YOUNG COMPARED TO MY BROTHER
AND SISTER SUNS, WHETHER NEARBY OR DISTANT,
BUT I HAVE STILL SEEN A LOT.
INDEED, AS YOU WELL KNOW, FEW OF MY
UNCOUNTABLE SIBLINGS HAVE HAD MY GOOD
FORTUNE—THE GOOD FORTUNE NOT TO TRAVEL
ALONE IN THE SEA OF SPACE.
VARIOUS WORLDS HAVE TAKEN SHAPE AROUND ME,
AND IN THE TIME I HAVE BEEN GRANTED THUS FAR,
I HAVE BEEN ABLE TO OBSERVE AND WITNESS MANY DIFFER-
ENT LIVES.

I AM GOING TO SHOW YOU SOME SCENES FROM
ONE OF THESE EXTRAORDINARY LIVES.
THEY ARE PART OF WHAT IS PERHAPS ONE OF THE
MOST EMOTIONAL SPECTACLES EVER STAGED BY EARTH,
THE JEWEL AMONG MY TRAVELING COMPANIONS.
YOU HUMANS HAVE BEEN ABLE TO DISCOVER LOST TRACES
OF THE HEROES OF THIS SPECTACLE: ROCK AMONG ROCKS, MOMENTS
OF STONE, FRAGMENTS OF A MOMENTOUS
SCENARIO THAT IS DIFFICULT TO RECONSTRUCT.
THE AGES HAVE TURNED THESE HEROES INTO MUTE STONES AND EMP-
TIED THEIR CHESTS OF BREATH AND WARMTH.

THIS IS MY MEMORY OF A PRIMITIVE SCENE THAT PLAYED OUT THOU-
SANDS AND THOUSANDS OF SEASONS AGO, BEFORE THE PYRAMIDS,
BEFORE THE GODS, BEFORE MAN'S APPEARANCE ON THE STAGE HAD
EVEN BEEN IMAGINED. I WILL TELL YOU ABOUT
THE CREATURES THAT LIVED DURING THIS TIME AS UNCONTESTED
RULERS, CONQUERING EVERY CORNER OF THE EARTH AND
ASSUMING THE WIDEST VARIETY OF FORMS.
THEY SEEMED INVINCIBLE, YET THEY MET WITH
A MYSTERIOUS END THAT TURNED THEM INTO
LEGEND. AND SO LET ME CONTINUE MY STORY.
I HAVE TOLD YOU ABOUT THE LONG JOURNEY, AT THE TIME OF THE NEW
TRACKS. I HAVE SPOKEN OF THE FINAL DAY IN THE LIFE OF A PRIMITIVE
BIRD WITH A HEAD OF SAPPHIRE BLUE DURING THE ERA OF ASCENT.
BENEATH SKIES DOMINATED BY WINGED LIZARDS, THIS ANCIENT PLUMED
ONE MANAGED TO SURVIVE
THE ATTACK OF HUNGRY PREDATORS AND THE RAGE OF
ARMORED CROCODILES.

IT WAS POWERLESS, HOWEVER, IN THE FACE OF A MONSOON AND, DRAGGED ALONG IN
THE WATERS, IT BECAME AN IMMORTAL MEMORY OF THE ORIGINS OF FEATHERED FLIGHT.
LISTEN NOW, AND LET MY WORDS CONJURE UP IMAGES OF HOW OTHER CREATURES OF
THIS AGE WALKED THE EARTH; HOW THEY WERE BORN, MIGRATED, AND DIED;
THE TASTES THEY SAVORED, AND THE NOISES THEY HEARD.
THIS TIME I WILL TELL YOU A STORY OF PASSION; A STORY ABOUT HUNTING, CLAWS,
AND FEROCIOUS TEETH; A STORY ABOUT NEW LEADERS AND DOMINATION.

3 THE HUNTING PACK

A DARK THICKET IN A LARGE PLAIN IS FULL OF THE RUMBLING OF SMALL CREATURES, CALLED INTO BEING BY THE ETERNAL SUMMER AT THE PEAK OF THE ERA OF ASCENT.

TWEET

TWEET

TWEET

KWEK

BUT THEIR VOICES FADE AWAY AND THEY RAPIDLY GROW SILENT...

TWEET

TWEET

KWEEK

KRACK

KWEEK

...WHEN FROM THE HEART OF THE FOREST THE ROAR OF BATTLE GROWS. SOMETHING LARGE AND MOMENTOUS IS APPROACHING.

THUMP

KRACK

THUD

THUD

KRACK!

DASH!

A CRY SHATTERS THE AIR AND A TREE CRASHES TO EARTH, AS A STOCKY, LONG-NECKED BEAST BURSTS INTO VIEW LIKE A FIREBALL FROM THE DARK TREES.

OTHERS FOLLOW.

STOMP

STOMP

STOMP

FOUR—NO, FIVE FIERCE BIPEDS GLIDE WITH CATLIKE ELEGANCE OUT OF THE VEGETATION. THEY ARE GAINING ON THEIR PREY.

THIS STORY UNFOLDS OVER A THOUSAND GENERATIONS AFTER OUR LAST MYSTERY... THE ERA OF ASCENT IS ENDING. STILL, WE ARE FAR FROM THE LAND OF THE ANCIENT WINGED ONE, IN THE IMMENSE WESTERN REGIONS OF WHAT YOU WILL CALL NORTH AMERICA.

THE PACK OF THREE-CLAWED ONES IS EATING; THE HUNT WAS SUCCESSFUL, WHICH NOT ALWAYS THE CA

LIKE EVERY PACK, THIS ONE HAS ITS LEADER:

THE POWERFUL, SCARLET-HORNED MALE DID NOT JOIN HIS CHILDREN AND WIVES IN THE HUNT, BUT HE EXPECTS TO EAT FIRST.

HE DEMA RESPEC FOR TH DOMINAN

ROAR!

...TO WHICH HIS SCARRED BODY BEARS WITNESS.

IT IS NOT ONLY THE OTHER HUNTERS THAT MUST WAIT:

A SMALL CROWD OF OPPORTUNISTS HAS GATHERED, LURED BY THE STRONG ODOR OF AN EASY MEAL.

THERE ARE STURDY HUNTERS WITH CRESTED FACES . . .

. . . WHO OFTEN HOPE TO FEAST ON THE REMAINS OF THE MEAL EATEN BY THE LARGER THREE-CLAWED ONES.

THERE ARE WINGED LIZARDS.

THERE ARE ALSO AGILE, PLUMED THIEVES, WHO SOMETIMES GIVE IN TO TEMPTATION . . .

NO PART OF THE PREY WILL GO TO WASTE.

THEY WILL ALL HAVE A TURN.

ALL OF THEM KNOW THAT IT IS BETTER TO WAIT UNTIL THE LARGE HUNTERS HAVE EATEN THEIR FILL.

. . . BUT PAY THE CONSEQUENCES!

19

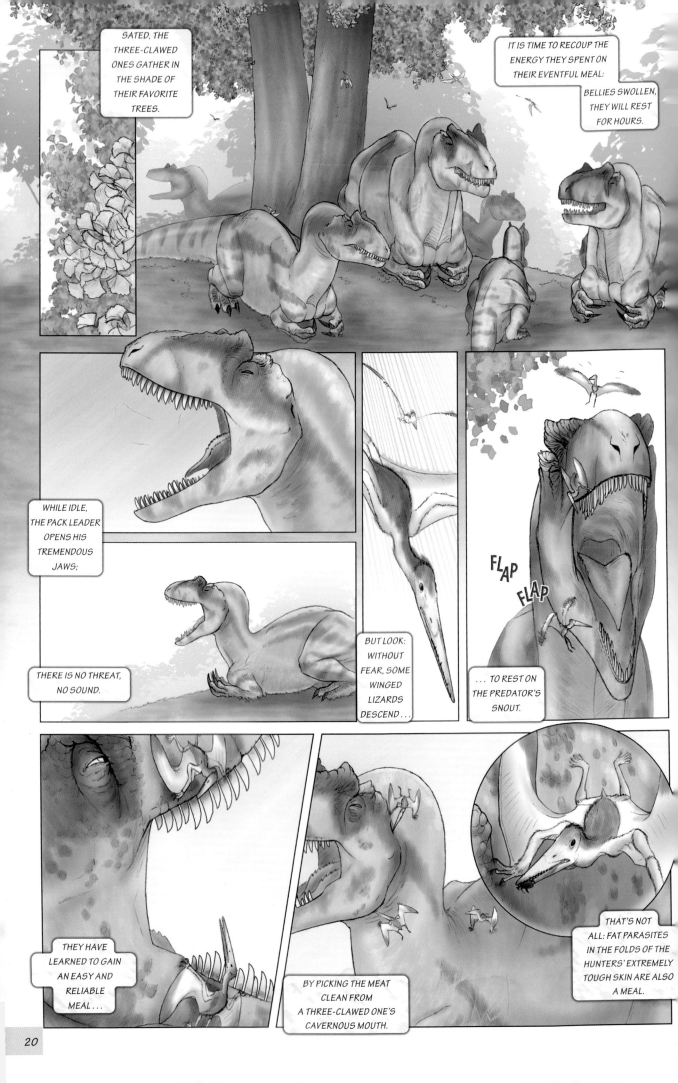

SATED, THE THREE-CLAWED ONES GATHER IN THE SHADE OF THEIR FAVORITE TREES.

IT IS TIME TO RECOUP THE ENERGY THEY SPENT ON THEIR EVENTFUL MEAL:

BELLIES SWOLLEN, THEY WILL REST FOR HOURS.

WHILE IDLE, THE PACK LEADER OPENS HIS TREMENDOUS JAWS;

THERE IS NO THREAT, NO SOUND.

BUT LOOK: WITHOUT FEAR, SOME WINGED LIZARDS DESCEND . . .

FLAP
FLAP

. . . TO REST ON THE PREDATOR'S SNOUT.

THEY HAVE LEARNED TO GAIN AN EASY AND RELIABLE MEAL . . .

BY PICKING THE MEAT CLEAN FROM A THREE-CLAWED ONE'S CAVERNOUS MOUTH.

THAT'S NOT ALL: FAT PARASITES IN THE FOLDS OF THE HUNTERS' EXTREMELY TOUGH SKIN ARE ALSO A MEAL.

SATED
'CNIVORES'
STING PLACE IS AT THE
OF A SMALL SLOPE.

FROM HERE, THE FIERCE PACK LEADER CAN RULE THE ENTIRE VALLEY.

SLEEPY, HE GLANCES AROUND AT:

THE LARGE, LOW PLAIN, TRAVERSED BY A MAJESTIC RIVER;

THE FORESTS OF TREES, ENORMOUS, EVEN FOR THESE GIGANTIC PREDATORS;

THE WHITE STONE PEAKS RISING FROM THE PLAIN LIKE PREHISTORIC STEEPLES.

SOME OF THE LARGEST ANIMALS THAT HAVE EVER LIVED INHABIT THESE LANDS.

AND ALONG THE EDGE OF THE LABYRINTHINE WOOD, IN THE DISTANCE . . .

. . . FEEDS A HERD OF THE MOST COLOSSAL DINOSAURS OF THE ERA.

OME SMALL VEGETARIAN
INOSAURS,
HICH YOU WILL
LL OAK
IZARDS, SCAMPER ABOUT
MONG THE MASSIVE LEGS
F THESE GIANTS.

OFTEN THEY
GATHER AROUND THE HERD
TO TAKE ADVANTAGE OF ITS
INDIRECT PROTECTION.

THEY GRAZE AMID THE
UNDERGROWTH AND FERNS,
TOO LOW FOR THEIR
ENORMOUS COMPANIONS;

UNLIKE THE NEARBY
TITANS, THEY ARE ABLE
TO CHEW, AND SO THEY
CAN FEED OFF ALMOST
ANY PLANT.

THEY ALSO PROFIT
FROM WHAT FALLS
FROM ABOVE.

UNFORTUNATELY ANOTHER GIANT HAS HAD THE SAME IDEA:

A WHIP-TAILED BEAST.

GROUP

OUR SHIELDED ONE PROTESTS.

S ACCIDENTAL TABLE MPANION CERTAINLY DOESN'T POSE ANY DANGER,

BUT THE IRRITABLE HERBIVORE SEES LITTLE AND REASONS LESS,

SO IT THREATENS ITS FELLOW BAN-QUETER WITH ITS SPIKED TAIL.

THE OTHER BEAST, DESPITE ITS GREAT SIZE, KNOWS WELL NOT TO STAY AND TEMPT FATE,

SO, WITH THE SLOWNESS THAT ITS HUGE FRAME IMPOSES,

IT MOVES IN STATELY FASHION TO GRAZE AT A POLITE DISTANCE.

25

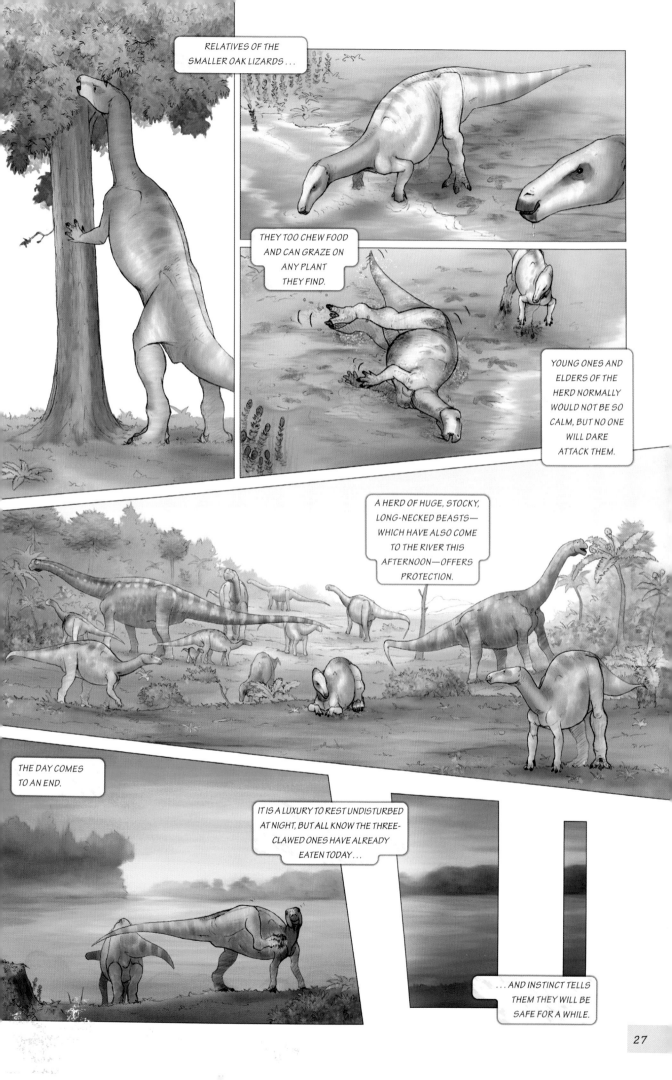

A NEW DAY:
THE PACK IS DOZING LAZILY.

THE HUNTERS LIKE TO LOLL ABOUT:

ONE OF THEM HINTS AT A YAWN, BUT THE LARGEST ARE HAPPY NOT TO MOVE FOR MANY HOURS TO COME.

THE YOUNGER ONES, THOUGH, ARE ALREADY MOVING, JUST LIKE THE LARGE PACK LEADER;

THE OLD MALE IS EXCITED BY THE SCENT COMING FROM ONE OF THE FEMALES.

MATING SEASON IS BEGINNING.

HE BELLOWS A CLUMSY LOVE SONG FOR HIS GIRL . . .

BUT SHE LE
HIM KNC
THAT SHE
STILL NOT WON OVE

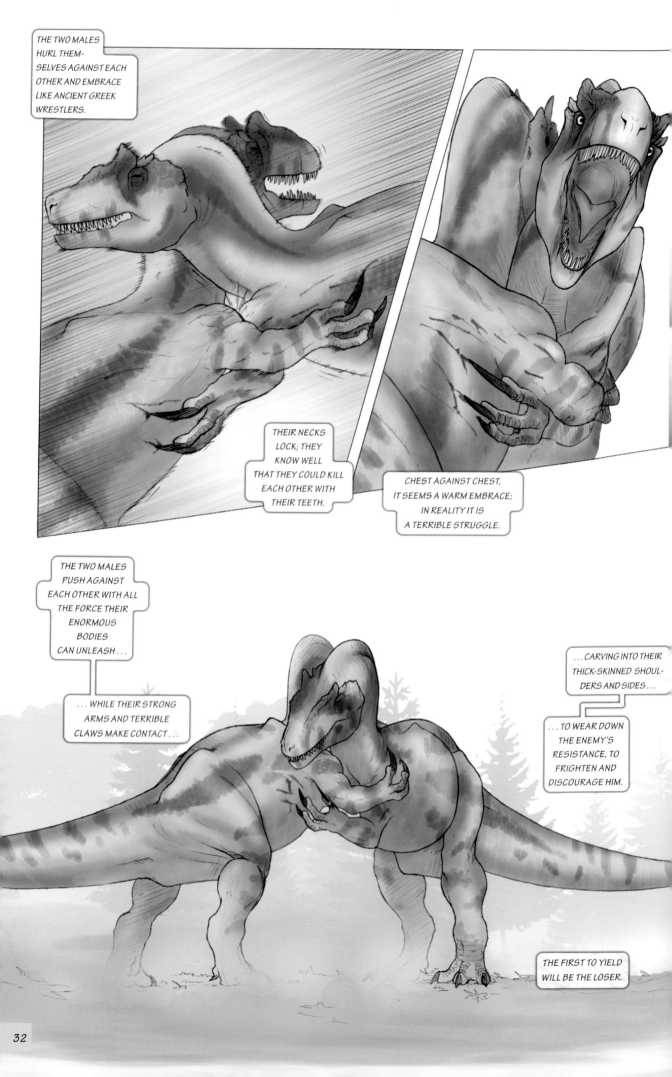

THE TWO MALES HURL THEM-SELVES AGAINST EACH OTHER AND EMBRACE LIKE ANCIENT GREEK WRESTLERS.

THEIR NECKS LOCK; THEY KNOW WELL THAT THEY COULD KILL EACH OTHER WITH THEIR TEETH.

CHEST AGAINST CHEST, IT SEEMS A WARM EMBRACE; IN REALITY IT IS A TERRIBLE STRUGGLE.

THE TWO MALES PUSH AGAINST EACH OTHER WITH ALL THE FORCE THEIR ENORMOUS BODIES CAN UNLEASH . . .

. . . WHILE THEIR STRONG ARMS AND TERRIBLE CLAWS MAKE CONTACT . . .

. . . CARVING INTO THEIR THICK-SKINNED SHOUL-DERS AND SIDES . . .

. . . TO WEAR DOWN THE ENEMY'S RESISTANCE, TO FRIGHTEN AND DISCOURAGE HIM.

THE FIRST TO YIELD WILL BE THE LOSER.

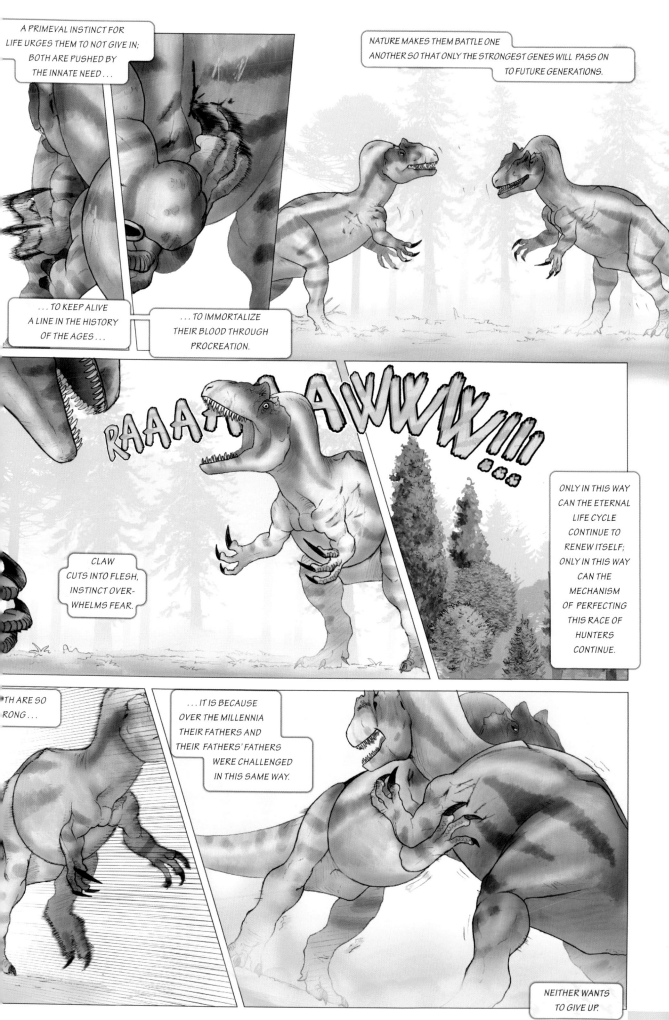

A PRIMEVAL INSTINCT FOR LIFE URGES THEM TO NOT GIVE IN; BOTH ARE PUSHED BY THE INNATE NEED...

NATURE MAKES THEM BATTLE ONE ANOTHER SO THAT ONLY THE STRONGEST GENES WILL PASS ON TO FUTURE GENERATIONS.

...TO KEEP ALIVE A LINE IN THE HISTORY OF THE AGES...

...TO IMMORTALIZE THEIR BLOOD THROUGH PROCREATION.

RAAAA AWW!!!

CLAW CUTS INTO FLESH, INSTINCT OVERWHELMS FEAR.

ONLY IN THIS WAY CAN THE ETERNAL LIFE CYCLE CONTINUE TO RENEW ITSELF; ONLY IN THIS WAY CAN THE MECHANISM OF PERFECTING THIS RACE OF HUNTERS CONTINUE.

TH ARE SO RONG...

...IT IS BECAUSE OVER THE MILLENNIA THEIR FATHERS AND THEIR FATHERS' FATHERS WERE CHALLENGED IN THIS SAME WAY.

NEITHER WANTS TO GIVE UP.

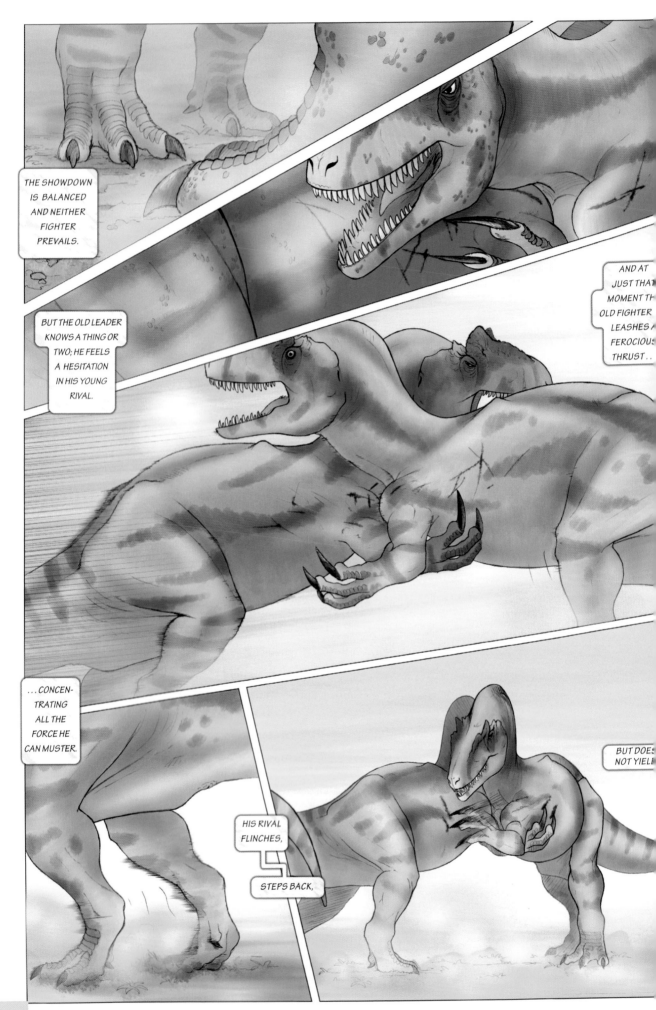

THE SHOWDOWN IS BALANCED AND NEITHER FIGHTER PREVAILS.

AND AT JUST THAT MOMENT THE OLD FIGHTER LEASHES A FEROCIOUS THRUST . . .

BUT THE OLD LEADER KNOWS A THING OR TWO; HE FEELS A HESITATION IN HIS YOUNG RIVAL.

. . . CONCEN-TRATING ALL THE FORCE HE CAN MUSTER.

BUT DOES NOT YIELD.

HIS RIVAL FLINCHES,

STEPS BACK,

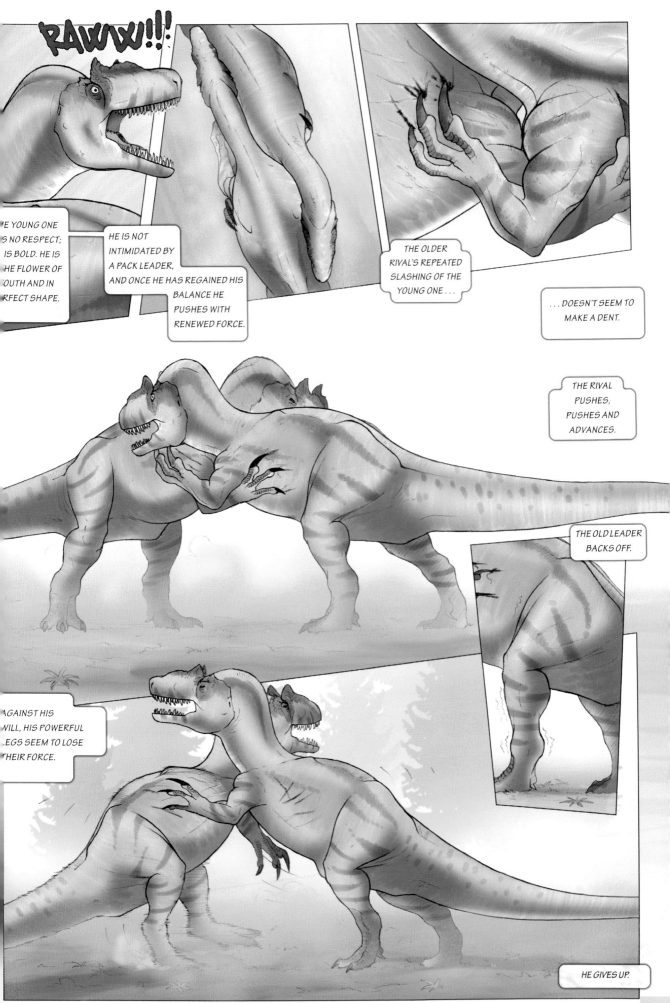

RAWW!!!

E YOUNG ONE
S NO RESPECT;
IS BOLD. HE IS
HE FLOWER OF
OUTH AND IN
RFECT SHAPE.

HE IS NOT
INTIMIDATED BY
A PACK LEADER,
AND ONCE HE HAS REGAINED HIS
BALANCE HE
PUSHES WITH
RENEWED FORCE.

THE OLDER
RIVAL'S REPEATED
SLASHING OF THE
YOUNG ONE . . .

. . . DOESN'T SEEM TO
MAKE A DENT.

THE RIVAL
PUSHES,
PUSHES AND
ADVANCES.

THE OLD LEADER
BACKS OFF.

AGAINST HIS
WILL, HIS POWERFUL
EGS SEEM TO LOSE
THEIR FORCE.

HE GIVES UP.

35

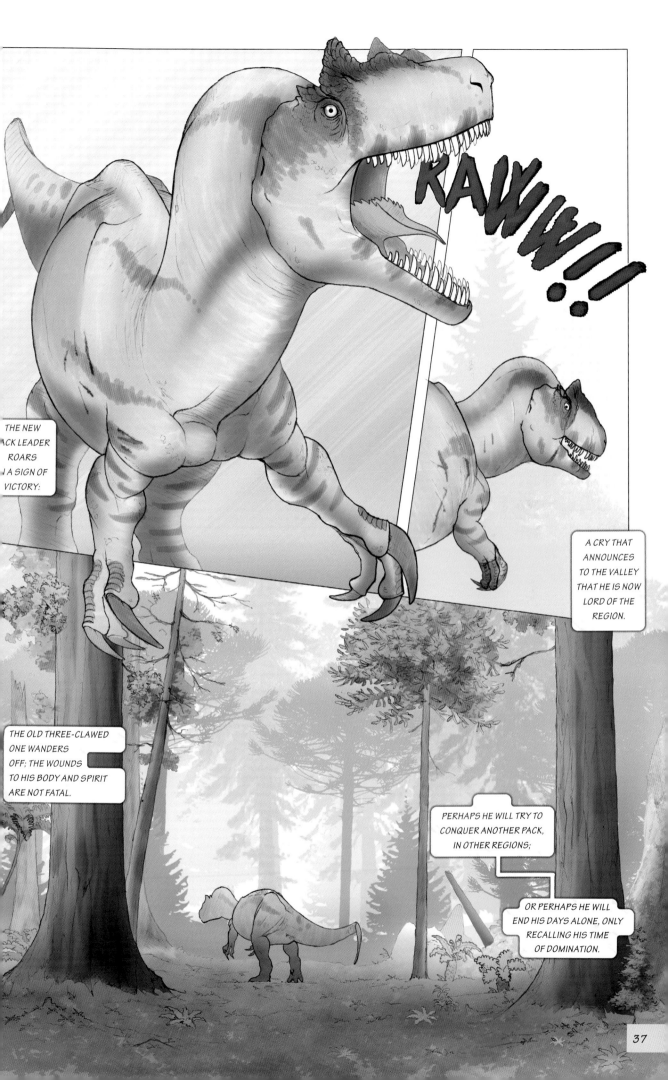

THE NEW PACK LEADER ROARS IN A SIGN OF VICTORY:

RAWW!!!

A CRY THAT ANNOUNCES TO THE VALLEY THAT HE IS NOW LORD OF THE REGION.

THE OLD THREE-CLAWED ONE WANDERS OFF; THE WOUNDS TO HIS BODY AND SPIRIT ARE NOT FATAL.

PERHAPS HE WILL TRY TO CONQUER ANOTHER PACK, IN OTHER REGIONS;

OR PERHAPS HE WILL END HIS DAYS ALONE, ONLY RECALLING HIS TIME OF DOMINATION.

THE YOUNG THREE-CLAWED ONE NOISILY SHOWS OFF TO HIS NEW COMPANIONS.

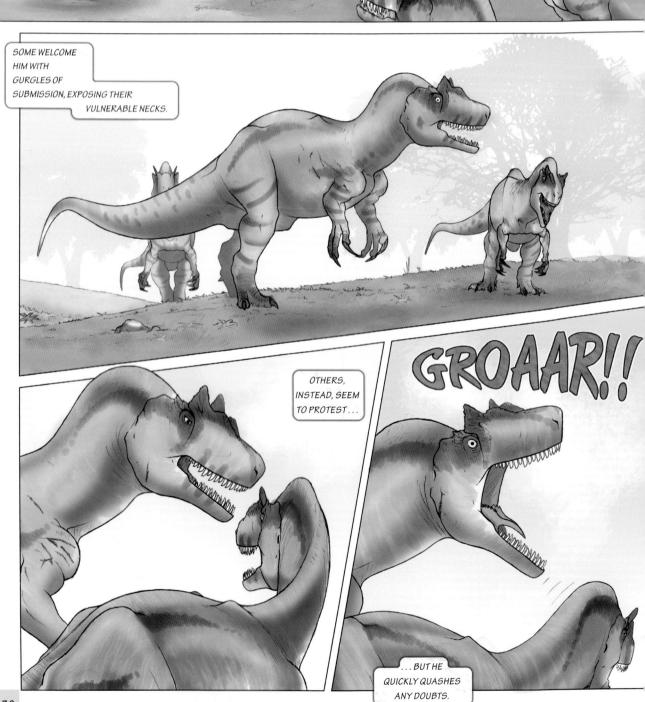

SOME WELCOME HIM WITH GURGLES OF SUBMISSION, EXPOSING THEIR VULNERABLE NECKS.

OTHERS, INSTEAD, SEEM TO PROTEST...

GROAAR!!

...BUT HE QUICKLY QUASHES ANY DOUBTS.

DINOSAUR EVOLUTION

This diagram of the evolution of the dinosaurs (in which the red lines represent evolutionary branches for which there is fossil evidence) shows the two principal groups (the saurischians and ornithischians) and their evolutionary path through time during the Mesozoic. Among the saurischians (to the right), we can see the evolution of the sauropodomorphs, who were all herbivores and were the largest animals ever to walk the earth. Farther to the right, still among the saurischians, we find the theropods. Among the theropods there quite soon emerges a line characterized by rigid tails (Tetanurae), from which, through the maniraptors, birds (Aves) evolve. The ornithischians (to the left), which were all herbivores, have an equally complicated evolutionary history, which begins with the basic Pisanosaurus type but soon splits into Thyreophora ("shield bearers," such as ankylosaurs and stegosaurs) on the one hand, and Genasauria ("lizards with cheeks") on the other. The latter in turn evolve into two principal lines: the marginocephalians, which include ceratopsians, and euornithopods, which include the most flourishing herbivores of the Mesozoic, the hadrosaurs.

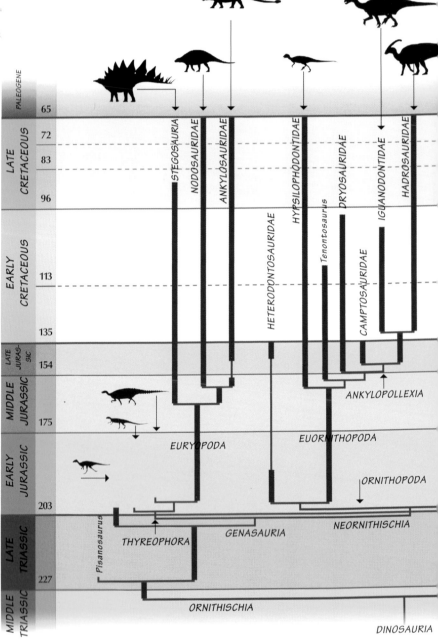

IDENTIKIT *(see page 6)*

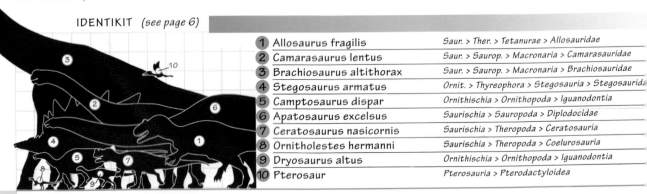

1	Allosaurus fragilis	Saur. > Ther. > Tetanurae > Allosauridae
2	Camarasaurus lentus	Saur. > Saurop. > Macronaria > Camarasauridae
3	Brachiosaurus altithorax	Saur. > Saurop. > Macronaria > Brachiosauridae
4	Stegosaurus armatus	Ornit. > Thyreophora > Stegosauria > Stegosauridae
5	Camptosaurus dispar	Ornithischia > Ornithopoda > Iguanodontia
6	Apatosaurus excelsus	Saurischia > Sauropoda > Diplodocidae
7	Ceratosaurus nasicornis	Saurischia > Theropoda > Ceratosauria
8	Ornitholestes hermanni	Saurischia > Theropoda > Coelurosauria
9	Dryosaurus altus	Ornithischia > Ornithopoda > Iguanodontia
10	Pterosaur	Pterosauria > Pterodactyloidea

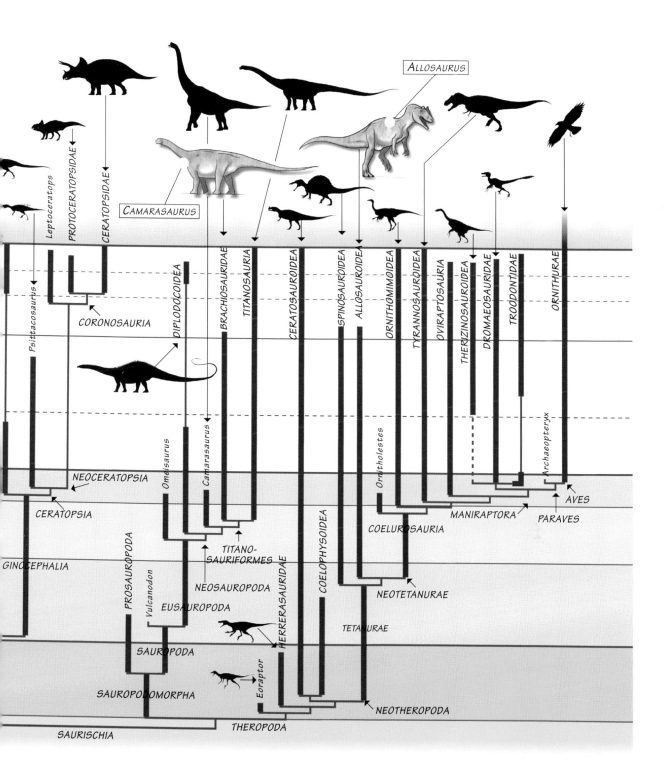

LENGTH	HEIGHT	WEIGHT	DIET	PERIOD	TERRITORY
over 40 feet	over 10 feet at the shoulder	over 4½ tons	meat	Late Jurassic (Kimmeridgian-Tithonian)	North America, Portugal
60 feet	over 13 feet at the shoulder	over 15 tons	vegetation	Late Jurassic (Kimmeridgian-Tithonian)	North America
up to 80 feet	up to 46 feet at the shoulder	over 60 tons	vegetation	Late Jurassic (Kimmeridgian-Tithonian)	North America, Africa
30 feet	over 13 feet at the shoulder	over 6 tons	vegetation	Late Jurassic (Kimmeridgian-Tithonian)	North America
23 feet	over 6½ feet at the shoulder	up to 3 tons	vegetation	Late Jurassic (Kimmeridgian-Tithonian)	North America
up to 85 feet	up to 16½ feet at the shoulder	up to 30 tons	vegetation	Late Jurassic (Kimmeridgian-Tithonian)	North America
over 20 feet	up to 6½ feet at the shoulder	over 1½ tons	meat	Late Jurassic (Kimmeridgian-Tithonian)	North America, Africa
6½ feet	over 1½ feet at the shoulder	up to 45 lbs.	meat	Late Jurassic (Kimmeridgian-Tithonian)	North America
over 11½ feet	over 3 feet at the shoulder	over 220 lbs.	vegetation	Late Jurassic (Kimmeridgian-Tithonian)	North America, Africa
wingspan: 6½ feet	unknown	unknown	meat and insects	Late Jurassic (Kimmeridgian-Tithonian)	North America

THE JURASSIC
THEY RULED
THE EARTH

The Morrison Formation

Our story is set in one of the world's most famous sites of dinosaur fossils: the Morrison Formation in the western United States.

This extremely vast area occupies several states, from Wyoming and Colorado—where the formation has its "center" and where the town of Morrison from which it takes its name is located— to ten other states, including Utah and Idaho.

Arthur Lakes, a fossil hunter who also dabbled in art, discovered the first dinosaur fossil here, in 1877. His watercolors provide incredibly vivid scenes of the search for fossils at the time of the Bone Wars, which we will discuss later.

The Morrison Formation is clearly extremely important and dates geologically to a period from 155 to 148 million years ago, at the end of the Jurassic period. The sediments that make up the formation were deposited over an enormous plain formed when the Sundance Sea, an epicontinental sea that extended through the present-day United States and Canada during the Jurassic, receded. In the southwestern portion, the Morrison sediments seem to be **aeolian** in origin, indicating that the area had a hot, arid desert climate. But farther north the sediments become **fluvial**; it appears that the plain was crisscrossed by large rivers, which deposited the debris and sediment they carried along on the flat terrain ✷**1**, and it is precisely in these alluvial deposits that fossils are found—including, of course, the bones of the gigantic dinosaurs that populate our story.

Given the wealth of the Morrison Formation, authorities have been quick to construct various research sites, and since the nineteenth century, quarries there have yielded the remains of dinosaurs and other animals.

Indeed, the fauna of the Morrison Formation includes more than dinosaurs. While the smallest bones are often fragmentary and sometimes unrecognizable, paleontologists have been able to reconstruct much of the animal life of these alluvial plains, which included pterosaurs, fish, salamanders, frogs, lizards, crocodiles, and small mammals. In some areas dinosaur eggs have also been discovered.

▼ *An image of the Morrison Formation in Colorado, showing the present-day barren terrain and plant life adapted to an arid climate.*

✷**1**
page 21
panel 3

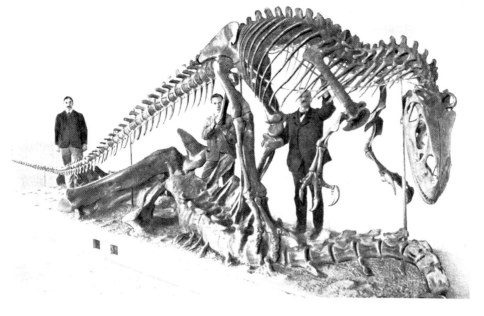

◀ The skeleton of Allosaurus fragilis, a reproduction of one assembled by famous paleontologist Henry Fairfield Osborn. This predator was reconstructed in the act of eating its prey, the bones of which can be glimpsed below those of the attacker. The mounting of this skeleton is surprisingly modern, attesting to the insightfulness of Osborn. (From www.search4dinosaurs.com)

However, the vast majority of finds consists of dinosaur bones. These remains are both abundant and well preserved, and in many places, such as Dinosaur National Monument, tourists can see bones still enclosed within rock, exactly as distinguished paleontologists such as Charles Marsh and Edward Cope first saw them, 150 years ago.

Of course, it is beyond the scope of this book to list in detail all the principal deposits of the Morrison Formation, but at least three sites merit a bit more attention. The first is Bone Cabin Quarry (near Laramie, Wyoming), where a local shepherd built a shelter entirely out of fossilized dinosaur bones. The discovery of this site in 1897 by the American Museum of Natural History in New York led to the unearthing of more than fifty partial dinosaur skeletons in a relatively small area. These include *Camarasaurus*, *Apatosaurus*, *Allosaurus*, and *Stegosaurus*, as well as the small carnivore *Ornitholestes*. The *Apatosaurus* discovered here was the first sauropod to be reassembled and mounted in the New York museum, in 1905.

Como Bluff (Laramie, Wyoming) is another area that is quite famous in the history of paleontology. The name of this site is derived from Lake Como, located to the west, which in turn takes its name from the more famous lake in Italy. In this deposit sauropods are also the most abundant fossils.

Finally, we must mention the Cleveland-Lloyd Dinosaur Quarry (Emery, Utah). While the first two sites were dominated by sauropods and herbivores in general, here *Allosaurus* alone accounts for approximately 75 percent of the finds, and this deposit contains almost exclusively dinosaur bones. This striking abundance of carnivore bones still amazes experts because, with the exception of specific sites—such as Ghost Ranch in Texas, which we discussed in the first book in this series—there are always fewer carnivores than herbivores in large accumulations of dinosaur bones.

As we have seen, the bones were deposited among sediments and then transported by rivers. Thus, not all animals discovered in the Morrison

◀ A long sauropod bone, displayed to the public just as it was found, in Dinosaur National Monument, U.S.A.

◀ Another view of the Morrison from Dinosaur National Monument, on a hot, windless day when the air was crystal clear.

Formation actually lived in that area; the rivers transported their carcasses and left them in protected bends or in cutoff channels, where the remains built up. In fact many areas of the Morrison Formation are actually masses of bones—*taphocenoses*, in technical jargon—that gradually formed as the rivers transported new carcasses to the same place. This type of phenomenon can still be seen today in large rivers, for example, after a flood, or in any case during a period when a river overflows its banks with debris in its waters, which then leaves a mark of the river's high water point. In areas that are not inhabited by man, the detritus remains where it accumulates, sometimes over many consecutive years, and the animal carcasses that are deposited along with it decompose, leaving behind only bones as a record of their passage. This is how, according to current ideas, the various Morrison Formation deposits developed. This type of fossilization can lead to interpretations that are not always correct about the ecology of the animals that were involved. For example, it was once thought that sauropods must have lived in rivers in order to support their enormous mass, and the discovery of their bones in fluvial sediments only encouraged this interpretation. Today we know that this was not the case at all, and that indeed it is likely that sauropods carefully avoided river areas, where they would have been in danger of getting stuck in the mud.

Before delving further into our exploration of the Morrison Formation of the Jurassic period, it is worthwhile to recall one of the most glorious and dramatic events in the history of paleontology: the Bone Wars. The leaders in this war were two of the greatest paleontologists who ever lived: Charles Othniel Marsh and Edward Drinker Cope.

This long war almost destroyed the two adversaries, along with their respective teams, but led to a great number of incredible discoveries—paleontologists today are still classifying and cataloguing the finds unearthed by the two "bone warriors"—resulting in the scientific descriptions of more than 140

◀ A portrait of Charles Othniel Marsh, protagonist in the Bone Wars of the late nineteenth century.

species of dinosaurs and more than 1,800 types of fossil vertebrates.

Cope and Marsh started out as close friends, but due to their personalities the relationship soon grew bitter; according to official sources the "war" broke out after Marsh publicly humiliated Cope by pointing out that the latter had incorrectly reconstructed the fossil of an *Elasmosaurus* (a plesiosaur), placing its head at the end of the tail!

Offended, Cope began digging in his former colleague's "private territories," and their relationship rapidly deteriorated. Beginning in 1858 their rivalry led to astounding scientific results, with tons upon tons of bones unearthed and transferred to museums, accompanied by accusations from both sides of spying, corruption, and stealing fossils and even each other's workers. The only victims of this incredible and for the most part bloodless war were the personal fortunes of the combatants, both of whom were extremely wealthy, but if a winner were to be declared, it would have to be Marsh, who described eighty-six new dinosaur species, while his antagonist, Cope, came up with "only" fifty-six.

Perhaps the real victims of this war were all the fossil skeletons that were destroyed by dynamite during excavations, or shattered when it proved impossible to transfer them to museums, to prevent the competing side from salvaging them. However, recent studies, carried out with the help of the detailed analysis of those paintings made by Arthur Lakes (remember?—the "discoverer" of the Morrison Formation), have shown that the most promising area of Como Bluff was not blown up by dynamite, but instead covered up by Lakes, who then spread rumors about the site's demolition with explosives in order to prevent Cope's men from digging in the same area. Lakes was obviously working for Marsh.

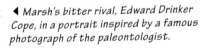

◀ Marsh's bitter rival, Edward Drinker Cope, in a portrait inspired by a famous photograph of the paleontologist.

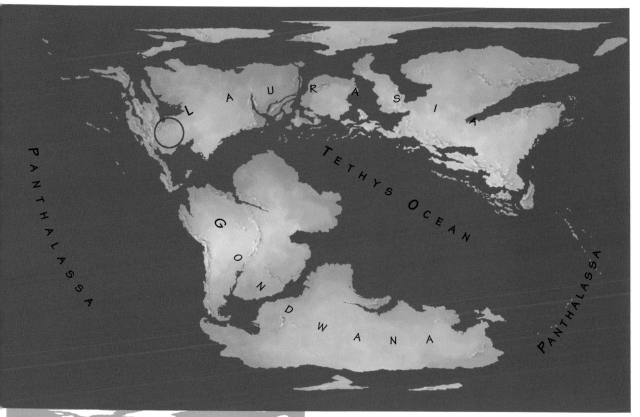

JURASSIC	**LATE**	Tithonian	141–135 million years ago
		Kimmeridgian	146–141 million years ago
		Oxfordian	154–146 million years ago
	MIDDLE	Callovian	160–154 million years ago
		Bathonian	164–160 million years ago
		Bajocian	170–164 million years ago
		Aalenian	175–170 million years ago
	EARLY	Toarcian	184–175 million years ago
		Pliensbachian	191–184 million years ago
		Sinemurian	200–191 million years ago
		Hettangian	203–200 million years ago

▲ The probable appearance of the planet during the Late Jurassic. A constant factor for almost the entire Mesozoic era was the compactness of Gondwana, while Laurasia tended to break up and become covered with epicontinental seas. The red circle indicates the location of the Morrison Formation in the present-day United States.

▶ Stratigraphic divisions of the levels of the Jurassic. It should be noted that in the United States the stratigraphy that is generally used has different details from the one used in Europe, which, however, is considered the standard. The Morrison is almost contemporary with Solnhofen, seen in the second book in this series, and our story takes place a bit later, in the Tithonian.

However much the story of Cope and Marsh inflamed paleontological circles throughout the world for decades, our story focuses instead on a more ancient war, the daily struggle for survival in the dinosaur world. The animals embedded in the fluvial sediments of the Morrison Formation were among the largest organisms ever to walk the earth. Our story introduces some of the best known, and in the following section, we will attempt to understand their anatomy, ecology, and, when possible, ethology or behavior.

The Dinosaurs of the Morrison Formation

Saurischians

The protagonist of this story is an *Allosaurus* *2, a large theropod that some people understandably refer to as "the tiger of the Jurassic." If we examine the skeleton of an *Allosaurus*, or one of its closest relatives in the Morrison Formation, such as *Saurophaganax*—which some believe is actually a larger species of the *Allosaurus* genus—we get a sense of the creature's power and agility, which were just like those of a modern-day tiger. But in this case we are speaking of a predator that could be thirty feet long or longer. The main weapon of this large predator was undoubtedly its skull, which had a sturdy but light structure, built for speed. Numerous cavities (windows) lightened the cranium but also gave it strength and elasticity. Its senses of smell and sight must have played an important role in the search for prey, and its

*2
page 18

▲ *Modern photo of an Allosaurus reconstruction in the American Museum of Natural History in New York; it must be emphasized that Osborn's reconstruction. seen on*

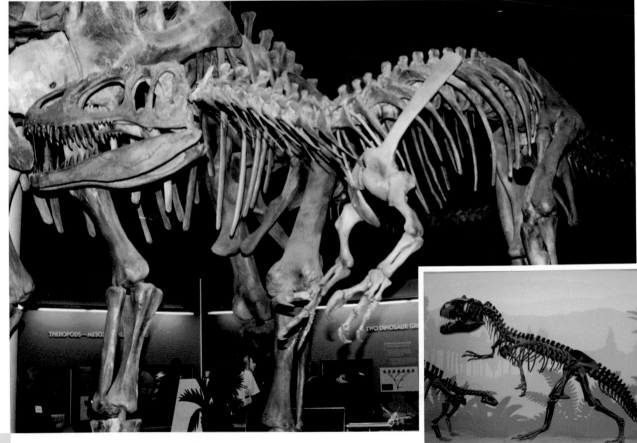

must have been a formidable offensive weapon. The rest of *Allosaurus*'s body, and those of related theropods in the allosaur group, was built for strength and balance. Its hands, which had three toes and large claws, were used to help catch prey, while the feet and tail acted as the animal's engine. There is a certain uniformity in the shape and proportions of the arms of theropods, and we know that many of them used these limbs for hunting. The largest of the carnivorous dinosaurs almost definitely employed their jaws as their principal weapon, but smaller predators, such as *Ornitholestes* or the Dromaeosauridae of the Cretaceous period, must have used their arms somewhat in the manner of mantises, which are modern predator insects. Indeed, if we analyze the main components of the front limbs of mantises and carnivorous dinosaurs, we discover that the proportions among the elements are extremely similar, as they come closer to dromeosaurs and to the line that would lead to birds. This can be explained by the similar way in which the parts functioned; small theropods might have used their hands in the same manner as mantises, or even modern eastern martial arts champions, with rapid and probably devastating attacks.

Allosaurus's powerful feet were capable of pushing it forward with speed and strength **✻3**; its tail was rigid and rather long and thus helped to balance the weight of its body's front portion, stabilizing the biped. The rigid tail is actually a **characteristic** of all advanced theropods, and this is why, beginning with the Allosauridae, paleontologists call advanced theropods Tetanurae, which can be translated as "rigid tails." The rigidity of the tail is fundamental. Think for a moment of acrobatics—tightrope-walking, for example; our typical image of the acrobat is a person holding a rigid pole. Tetanurae probably used their rigid tails like that pole to maintain their balance, since they had to stand on only two feet, and especially since the front of their bodies was quite heavy. A rigid tail would also be extremely helpful when the animal moved. Think of a boat's rudder, a rigid blade used to change direction on the water. It is possible that the rigid tail of Tetanurae functioned in the same way, perhaps during brief bursts of speed or sprints.

What do we know about *Allosaurus*'s social life? Not much. Paleontologists think that these animals may have hunted in packs **✻4**, which is plausible, especially considering the type of prey found in the Morr herbivores were not very common, so most animals that might have served as food for *Allosaurus* were well

✻3
page 15
panel 1

◄▼ *Details of* Allosaurus. *Left, the cranium, where it is possible to see the supraorbital crests and the cranial structure, greatly lightened by the windows, which made the animal's head simultaneously rapid and robust. Below, a detail of the predator's arm, with three enormous claws and the bony crests that bring to mind large, powerful muscles.*

◄ *Saurophaganax (Sam Noble Museum, Oklahoma), and in the small photo, an* Allosaurus. *The two animals are extremely similar, and some scholars feel it is not justifiable to divide these finds into two different genera.*

protected and often huge. Later we will see how the tank-like defenses of a *Stegosaurus* could make hunting it unpleasant for *Allosaurus*, but stalking sauropods could not have been an agreeable task either. The difference in size between predators and prey was enormous, and adult sauropods probably did not have natural enemies. Instead, as we have seen in our story, it is more likely that allosaurs hunted young sauropods, which would have been more "reasonable" in size.

The behavior of a pack of allosaurs may have been similar to that of a pack of present-day large cats, such as lions. The pack may have been ruled by a dominant adult, and perhaps—as in today's lion prides—the young males, having reached a certain age, would have abandoned the group to go in search of a new one. In fact, the end of our story features a clash between two males, something that was undoubtedly rather common among allosaurs. The clash must have been violent but not particularly bloody, and perhaps the large claws on the front feet were used much more frequently for these types of battles than for hunting ✳5. The loser was almost certainly forced to abandon the group and would have tried to form another one. Its only other option would have been to become a solitary hunter, which would not have been an easy existence.

Another thing we see in our story, and we cannot emphasize this enough, is that carnivores in general—and in all likelihood this is also true for theropods—did not spend their lives hunting. While hunting was extremely important for sustenance, most of their time was spent resting ✳6, because hunting is a

✳4
page 17
panel 4

▶ Torvosaurus, another predator of the Jurassic, less famous than Allosaurus but equally dangerous. This image shows that, while the front limbs were sturdy and well "armed," the principal weapon of these theropods was undoubtedly their powerful and precise bite, produced by a cranium that was robust yet light and equipped with knife-sized, serrated teeth that easily cut through flesh.

✳5
page 33
panel 1/2

tiring activity that does not always result in success. And so "catching one's breath" is fundamental for a carnivore. Lions and leopards, for example, still behave this way on the African plains, and the same conditions almost definitely would have limited the large predators on the plains of the Jurassic period.

While *Allosaurus* is the best-known and most frequently discovered carnivore in the Morrison Formation, it is not the only one. A supporting actor in our story, and undoubtedly one of the most interesting carnivores of the Jurassic, is *Ornitholestes*. It was much smaller than *Allosaurus*, had weaker teeth, and had a structure built for speed. Until a short time ago we knew relatively little about *Ornitholestes*, but it has recently been reexamined, and one of its most famous characteristics is now known to be an error, making historical illustrations inaccurate. Previously *Ornitholestes* ✳7 was depicted with a sort of horn on its nose, but recent studies have shown that this presumed horn is only a mistaken interpretation of a broken bone in the fossil.

Another, sometimes larger carnivore has been made famous by the Morrison remains. This is *Ceratosaurus* ✳8, a large, primitive theropod that does in fact have a distinctive rounded horn on its nose. This animal was a Late Jurassic "survivor," a direct descendant of primitive theropods such as *Liliensternus* (which we have met previously). *Ceratosaurus* is also only a secondary actor in our story, and we know very little about this creature, unlike *Allosaurus*. What is certain is that it was a more basic theropod; many of its structures, such as a not completely rigid tail and four-toed feet, were fairly primitive. These characteristics, along with features that clearly distinguish it from more ancient dinosaurs, make the taxonomic position of *Ceratosaurus* a nightmare for paleontologists who are concerned with systematic categories. However, even this large carnivore has played a glorious role in the popular imagination and has appeared in various films, including Walt Disney's *Fantasia* (in which *Ornitholestes* also appears).

Another large carnivore, *Torvosaurus*, was also discovered in the Morrison Formation; paleontologists have estimated that it was larger than the average *Allosaurus*, always assuming that the gigantic *Saurophaganax* is a different genus. *Torvosaurus* remains are relatively rare, leading paleontologists to hypothesize that, despite its estimated size, this large carnivore was not the **super-predator** of the Morrison. Some scholars believe that *Allosaurus* was superior because of its adaptation to hunting in packs, but since we do not know with certainty about the hunting habits of the other great carnivores, the less frequent occurrence of *Torvosaurus* remains could easily be explained by other causes, such as a habitat more removed from the large Morrison rivers and less **postmortem** transportation by these waterways as a result. The morphological characteristics of *Torvosaurus* position it in a different group from *Allosaurus*, and its classification is still somewhat uncertain. It was endowed with a massive cranium, relatively small front limbs, and a long, nonrigid tail like that of other tetanaurans.

We can conclude this discussion of theropods by mentioning other small carnivorous dinosaurs that have been discovered in the Morrison. *Coelurus* and *Tanycolagreus* are theropods comparable to *Ornitholestes*—in fact, until 2005 *Tanycolagreus* remains had been identified as those of *Ornitholestes*—and endowed with well-developed hands and a rigid tail; they were built for agility and speed. Moreover, the remains of two possible troodontids have been recently identified; these are small carnivores characterized by numerous unusually shaped teeth and very highly developed eyes and ears. Until now the fossil record of the Troodontidae family was limited to the Cretaceous period, but these sorts of discoveries push back the time of the appearance of these small theropods.

We have mentioned super-predators and hunting, but what was the ecological relationship between prey and predators in the Morrison Formation? Unfortunately, the answer, once again, is uncertain. For the taphonomic reasons described earlier, the Morrison deposits do not provide reliable information on the composition of local fauna. This is because the waterborne transport of carcasses occurs completely by chance. For example, if we look at the situation of the Cleveland-Lloyd Quarry, as noted in the

✳6
page 20
panel 2

✳7
page 19
panel 4

✳8
page 19
panel 2

introductory paragraph, we see that *Allosaurus* alone makes up approximately 75 percent of the fossils that have been discovered there. To put it briefly, this means that in that site there are at least three predators for every prey—assuming that the remaining 25 percent of the fossils belong to herbivores, which is not always the case. We know that this proportion is not at all natural; prey are normally much more numerous than predators, since the population of the hunted must compensate for the high number of losses experienced by the hunter. On the other hand, a small number of prey in relation to many predators means that the predator population would soon become extinct, since there would not be enough for it to eat. Another thing should also be noted: the relationship between prey and predators is not a simple one. In the Morrison, for example, *Allosaurus* is not the only predator; as we have seen, there are various other theropods—and a similar situation characterizes every terrestrial ecosystem, in every era. Most people are accustomed to thinking of the relationships between prey and predators as a sort of chain, or at most as a pyramid, in which there is a precise, direct line between the predator and the creature preyed upon. But natural systems are subject to an **alimentary regime** that should be pictured as an extremely complicated interwoven network. There are predators on different levels; in the Morrison, for example, we might imagine *Allosaurus* as a super-predator, then *Ceratosaurus* and *Torvosaurus* as lower-level predators, and below them the smaller theropods, such as *Coelurus*, *Ornitholestes*, *Tanycolagreus*, and the troodontids. In reality there is no well-defined "pecking order" among these animals, because fossil remains do not give us clear information about their distribution over their territory, or **home range**. Moreover, we cannot clearly identify each animal's prey. *Allosaurus* hunted young sauropods, as in our story, and we can guess that *Ceratosaurus* preferred to attack *Dryosauruses* ✱**9**. However, we know nothing about the prey of small theropods such as *Ornitholestes*. And when we examine this from the side of possible prey, things become even more confused. We can imagine that *Dryosaurus* or *Camptosaurus* might have presented an easy meal for large hunters or for a pack of *Coeluruses*. An adult sauropod or an enraged *Stegosaurus* would be an entirely different proposition. And yet we know that there was also a system of population control for *Stegosauruses*; otherwise we would have found only *Stegosaurus*

remains in the Morrison. However, we cannot know precisely what this system was.

Defining an entire ecosystem from the scant and fragmentary information of the fossil record becomes an almost impossible undertaking. We can come up with only an approximate portrayal of what actually occurred in the Morrison. And this is what we have tried to represent in our story.

As we saw at the beginning, the most prevalent creatures in the Morrison Formation were surely sauropods (despite the fact that they were herbivores!). Their distinctive characteristics are an extremely long neck with many vertebrae; a rather small head equipped with teeth of equal size, usually in the front portion of the mouth; four columnar legs; five-toed feet with few bones and often with one or two large claws; and usually a long tail that tended to balance out the front portion of the body.

Sauropods descended from prosauropods, animals such as the *Plateosaurus* discussed in the first book in our series; their bodies tended to be truly gigantic (although there were dwarf sauropods that grew to a length of "only" sixteen to twenty feet). Indeed, one can say that the era of true giants began precisely in the Jurassic period of

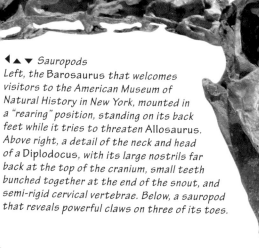

✱9
page 23
panel 2

✱10
page 25
panel 4

✱11
page 14
panel 5

✱12
page 22
panel 2

◄▲▼ *Sauropods*
Left, the Barosaurus *that welcomes visitors to the American Museum of Natural History in New York, mounted in a "rearing" position, standing on its back feet while it tries to threaten* Allosaurus. *Above right, a detail of the neck and head of a* Diplodocus, *with its large nostrils far back at the top of the cranium, small teeth bunched together at the end of the snout, and semi-rigid cervical vertebrae. Below, a sauropod that reveals powerful claws on three of its toes.*

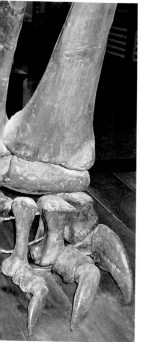

he Morrison Formation. Sauropods—animals of colossal dimensions, which had no equal, past or present, on earth—are probably the epitome of the dinosaur. When we think of the word "dinosaur," the first image that comes to mind is he placid, enormous apatosaur: four legs, long eck, long tail. While *Apatosaurus* ✱10 is a well-nown name, surely everyone, at least once, has eard of *Brontosaurus*, the "thundering lizard." And et this "reptile of thunder" is actually *Apatosaurus*!

This unusual situation is the result of a story hat dates back to the era of the Bone Wars. Marsh was the first person to describe *Apatosaurus* nd then *Brontosaurus*, but shortly thereafter it was hown that the bones of the two animals were too imilar to justify two different genera. Therefore, nce the **International Code of Zoological Nomenclature** states that the first name to

be published has precedence over all later names, today the genus is called *Apatosaurus*, and *Brontosaurus* is only a "synonym."

Like all sauropods, *Apatosaurus* was a very large quadruped animal (adults were sixty-five to seventy-five feet long), with a long neck and a long tail. The *Apatosaurus* cranium was not originally identified among the discovered remains, and so, when the gigantic skeleton was reassembled, paleontologists mistakenly attached the head of a *Camarasaurus*. This led to a series of significant errors, as a result of which *Apatosaurus* was always reconstructed with the head of another animal until the early 1980s, when the original head was found and positioned on the skeleton. Thousands of illustrations had to be changed! *Camarasaurus* ✱11, the animal to which the "spare" head belonged, is another Morrison Formation sauropod; at the beginning of our story we see it being hunted down by allosaurs. As part of the Morrison "loot," this sauropod also fell victim to the Bone Wars between Cope and Marsh. Its name was much debated because the first remains that were discovered (in 1877) were limited to just a few vertebrae. The first complete *Camarasaurus* was not discovered until 1925, and it was a fossil of a young animal; this is precisely why in many depictions of this dinosaur, dating back to the first half of the twentieth century, it appears to be fairly small. The strangest thing, if one thinks about these two facts, is that in reality *Camarasaurus* (the name, for the record, means "reptile with chambers") was probably the most widespread of the Morrison sauropods.

In our story there is also another sauropod, the remains of which are more common in Africa but are also found in the Morrison. This animal is quite different from the first two and is somewhat squatter and taller: *Brachiosaurus* ✱12. As fans of dinosaur films know, *Brachiosaurus* had the honor of appearing in *Jurassic Park*, and so its general appearance is very familiar even to those who only occasionally take an interest in dinosaurs. It is a colossal animal with a vertical neck, rather than the horizontally configured neck of the other two sauropods mentioned here. Moreover, its front legs are much longer than its rear legs (indeed, its name means "reptile with arms"); it also has a stubby tail.

Sauropods have been the subject of both myth and scientific speculation ever since their enormous skeletons appeared in museums. The first myth—and seemingly the most difficult to get those who are not well acquainted with paleontology to forget—is that sauropods lived in the water. As we have already seen, the taphonomy of the Morrison Formation may have contributed to this myth, but generally speaking, the size and estimated weight of these animals has always made them "too large" for the human imagination; even recent films (specifically *Jurassic Park*) have unfortunately contributed to this error in interpretation. Today we know with certainty that the skeletal and structural features of these animals allowed them grow to incredible size; according to some scholars the largest sauropods were more than 130 feet long and weighed more than 132 tons. Their spinal column was constructed like a T-beam used in the frames of large present-day buildings, and therefore allowed considerable shifting of the stress caused by the animal's weight. A system of enormous tendons and the lightening of the bones with cartilage also permitted these animals to walk easily over solid terrain. Indeed, according to many paleontologists, sauropods avoided swampy or, in any case, watery areas because they might have become trapped there, and thus could have become easy prey for theropods.

Another myth connected to sauropods, which has become controversial over time for scholars in this field, is the position of their neck. For decades sauropods have been depicted with their necks held high in a curved line, like those of swans. But recent studies have demonstrated that most sauropods held their necks parallel to the ground ✱13 and almost never lifted them up. This was because the cervical vertebrae had systems of blocks that prevented the neck from extending upward. (One exception to this general rule is the group that includes *Brachiosaurus*, which as far as we can tell *was* able to hold its neck almost straight up.) Their tails were held high and parallel to the ground, almost certainly to balance the weight of their necks. In some cases sauropod necks reached improbable lengths (as in the case of the *Mamenchisaurus*, a sauropod that lived in what is now China). But in general, almost all sauropods had rather long necks with small heads.

The posture of the neck has now led some paleontologists to hypothesize that different types of sauropods may have grazed at varying heights. Sauropods with practically horizontal necks, such as *Apatosaurus*, must have found food in lower vegetation ✱14. Animals such as *Camarasaurus*, which had a somewhat higher neck, would have been able to gather vegetation at a medium height ✱15. Finally, *Brachiosaurus* would have been able to feed like a present-day giraffe, directly from the treetops ✱16.

In 1986 Bob Bakker, an audacious and controversial paleontologist, proposed a truly original theory to explain the enormous nostrils of some sauropods. In fact, the nostrils of these animals are positioned virtually on the forehead—another circumstance that encouraged the theory of aquatic sauropods. In many cases, the nostrils are so large that paleontologists named this classification of animals Macronaria, which means "large nostrils."

Bakker's comparison of sauropods with certain present-day animals, including tapirs and elephants, led him to suggest the idea that they had trunks. We must admit that this idea is truly fascinating, but the paleontological world gave it a cool reception and scant consideration. Unfortunately, to demonstrate the presence or absence of a structure like a trunk in a dinosaur would require either an absurd stroke of good luck—a sauropod with preserved soft parts—or a time machine! In any case, it should be mentioned that in a recent analysis of the cranium fossil of a sauropod, paleontologists found no trace of the muscles or nerve canals that are normally associated with a trunk.

However, sauropods did have a wide array of special features related to their diet, metabolism, and even the laying of eggs. In fact, we know from fossil remains that most sauropods swallowed their food whole—their diet consisted of plants, probably entire branches torn off from low trees—and then ground it up in their particularly muscular stomachs, with the help of stones! Somewhat like modern birds, sauropods swallowed stones and used them to help with digestion. We can deduce this from numerous discoveries of these stones—known as *gastroliths*, which are perfectly smooth and polished by the digestive juices—in the rib cages of sauropods, more or less where the stomach must have been located.

Another subject that has been much debated concerns sauropods and the type of **metabolism** that such large animals must have had. Today many paleontologists tend to explain any dinosaur characteristic by invoking the example of birds; accordingly, some scholars think that sauropods had a metabolism similar to that of birds, and that they had **air sacs** that allowed them to breathe. It is clear that sauropod skeletons are highly pneumatic—that is, they have "hollow" bones—and these bony spaces were probably filled with such air sacs.

For now, the degree to which these sacs were used for breathing remains the object of speculation, and many current theories are unconvincing despite being very much in fashion. We can hypothesize that the mechanism known as gigantothermy, or inertial **homeothermy**, as it is often

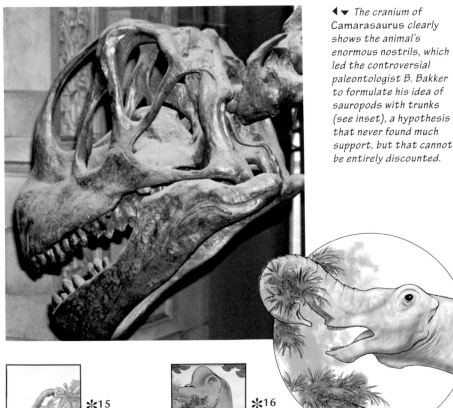

◀ Mamenchisaurus, the "reptile of the Mâmíngxi ferry," in China. Its neck is among the longest—if not the longest—in the history of vertebrates, and could reach a length of over 35 feet. The name of this sauropod comes from the place where it was first discovered, a construction site near the Mâmíngxi ferry. The species M. constructus *was also established to commemorate its discovery at a construction site.*

◀▼ The cranium of Camarasaurus *clearly shows the animal's enormous nostrils, which led the controversial paleontologist B. Bakker to formulate his idea of sauropods with trunks (see inset), a hypothesis that never found much support, but that cannot be entirely discounted.*

✳13
page 26
panel 1

✳14
page 26
panel 5

✳15
page 27
panel 4

✳16
page 22
panel 4

called, can provide some answers to the question of sauropods' metabolism, but unfortunately not to that of their breathing. What is this theory? Despite the complicated name, the concept is extremely simple. Beginning with the assumption that sauropods were **ectothermic** animals—in other words, that their body temperature, like that of reptiles, was based on the temperature of the surrounding environment—the model centers on the fact that a large mass takes a long time to change temperature. This happens because as an animal gradually increases in size, the surface of exchange, the skin, increases by a factor of two, while the volume increases by a factor of three.

Simply put, the surface increases less than the volume; the less the increase (the larger the animal becomes), the more the available radiant surface decreases, and the more the thermal exchanges diminish in turn. For enormous masses, such as those of sauropods, the thermal exchange becomes extremely inefficient, and so the animal tends to heat up or cool down very slowly. The climates that animals such as sauropods lived in during the Jurassic remained quite constant, and once their body temperature reached an optimum level, it would have taken an extremely long time for it to change. Since the environmental temperature changed so little, the animal's temperature remained at a more or less constant level. So even though some animals were ectothermic, their great mass would actually keep them homeothermic.

Finally, we also know something about sauropods' reproductive strategies. Many paleontologists, studying the footprint tracks attributed to these dinosaurs, have developed the idea that these gigantic animals lived in herds **∗17**, protecting their young by keeping them on the inside of the "formation" when they were on the move—and perhaps also while they were eating—while adults remained on the outside. This system offered the small creatures the protection of a self-propelled "stockade," the adults' legs, through which carni-

vores could not pass. (Isolating a young dinosaur would have been the only reasonable tactic for predators of these enormous creatures.) Moreover, discoveries in Argentina, which will be discussed further in book five in this series, have led paleontologists to theorize that sauropods laid their eggs in linear nests, that is, one egg at a time, arranged in an almost straight line.

Thus sauropods provide perhaps one of the best examples of how, beginning with a skeleton and some footprints, paleontologists can carry out their work like Sherlock Holmeses of prehistory, explaining the life and behavior of animals that none of us has ever seen, or presumably ever will see, alive.

▼ *Sauropod necks. A* Diplodocus, *below, and, below left, a* Camarasaurus. *It should be noted that the perfectly wedged vertebrae did not make the neck flexible, as was once generally thought. Moreover, it is possible to see two different cranial structures: more elongated and with smaller teeth in* Diplodocus, *and shorter, more open, and with larger teeth in* Camarasaurus.

∗17
pages 22, 2
panels 5, 1,

Ornithischians

Until now our stories have had saurischian dinosaurs as their main characters. In the Morrison Formation we will finally get to know, close up, the second large **clade**, or branch, of dinosaurs: ornithischians. As you may recall from our first book, dinosaurs are divided into two large groups based on the structure of the pelvis, namely the three bones that form the pelvic girdle where hind limbs are connected: the ilium, the ischium, and the pubis. The pelvic girdle is the most obvious difference between saurischians and ornithischians, but there are other differences that help to better identify the second group.

First of all, there is the skull, the body part in which, as in all vertebrates, differences become most evident. The ornithischian cranium has two more bones than that of a saurischian, in this case the palpebral bone on the eye socket and a premandibular bone in front of the lower jaws. The extra jawbone becomes very important because it acts along with the premaxillary bones as a sort of beak—one that is present in all ornithischians, probably even the most primitive. The teeth are also important in the classification of ornithischians; they are often positioned relatively far back in the jaw, and in ornithopods—the most common group of ornithischians—they take on different shapes depending on where they are located in the mouth. Indeed, an animal such as *Heterodontosaurus* has three types of teeth, which, upon close examination, resemble those of mammals: teeth shaped like incisors in the front part of the mouth; canine teeth, perhaps used in combat between males of the same species, or as an extreme defensive weapon against predators; and back teeth in the shape of molars, for chewing plants. (The presence of an anterior beak and teeth positioned relatively far back in the mouth once suggested to paleontologists that these animals may also have had cheeks, which prevented plants from falling out of the mouth during **food processing**. However, the careful analysis of a group of scientists led by Lawrence M. Witmer of Ohio University has shown that this is not the case.) Teeth for grinding then led to a spectacular innovation in the diet of these animals, which we will discuss shortly.

The remains of ornithischian skeletons also exhibit important differences from those of saurischians. In addition to the shape of the pelvic girdle, you can observe a clear tendency toward a four-footed posture in all ornithischi-

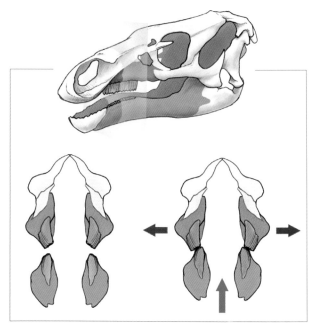

▲ *Pleurokinesis in ornithopods: the colored portions of the skull are the parts that are principally involved in movement. In practice, when the dentary (blue) rises, the maxillary bone (red) moves outward, allowing the opposing sets of teeth to scrape against each other and function as a "mill" for grinding plants. This system of mastication or chewing was successful and became enormously widespread throughout the Cretaceous period.*

▲ *The typical ornithischian pelvis (here one belonging to a Stegosaurus), with the ischium and pubis parallel and turned toward the rear portion of the animal's body.*

ans—with the exception of a few primitive and specialized forms, including the spectacular *Pachycephalosaurus*, which we will encounter in the last book in our series. Even potentially two-footed animals, such as the ornithopods of the Morrison (more about them to follow), usually moved about on four limbs. The tail is almost always massive, and there is often a system of intersecting tendons all along the spinal column, which would have allowed the animal to maintain a position almost horizontal to the ground, its tail held high. The front feet of ornithischians usually have five toes—though there are many variations, usually the result of local adaptations—while the rear feet can sometimes have only three or four toes. Finally, apart from the already noted exception of certain ceratopsids—ornithischian dinosaurs from the Cretaceous period that were endowed with horns and crests, and that we will discuss at length in book six—ornithischians were all herbivores, another substantial difference between them and saurischians.

Two Morrison ornithopods are represented in our story, but others are known from more or less fragmentary remains. The first that we will encounter is *Dryosaurus* ✳18 (the "oak reptile," because its teeth vaguely resemble the leaves of an oak tree): a relatively small animal (on average ten feet long and five feet high at the shoulder) with a light cranium, a beak at the end of the jawbones, and teeth that resemble the molars of mammals. This herbivore could rip up plants—or gather those dropped by grazing brachiosaurs, as in our story—and chew them. Thus we see another step forward in dinosaur evolution: chewing, the great innovation that we mentioned earlier. In fact, until the Jurassic period herbivores were limited to swallowing plants, sometimes cutting them up before placing them in their mouths, but nothing more. Our sauropods, as we have seen, swallowed stones to assist in digestion. Ornithopods were decidedly more "refined"; not content to rip up plants and swallow them, they chewed them instead. Clearly mastication in early ornithopods such as these *Dryosauruses* was not perfect, and was limited to the chewing of food with teeth similar to molars, probably with the help of muscular tongues. But as we will soon see, much more sophisticated animals were already appearing during the Jurassic. For the moment we will spend a bit more time with our dryosaurs and imagine them moving about on two or four legs—in fact, they were what we call facultative bipeds, meaning that they could walk on either two or four legs—amid the low vegetation of the Morrison. Speed, and probably their grouping in herds, must have been their only defenses.

✳18
page 23
panel 1

▲ *A herd of gnus. Like these present-day herbivores, plant-eating dinosaurs also lived in herds to protect themselves from predators. And just as large numbers of gnus can die while fording rivers, many herbivorous dinosaurs may have met a similar end, as seen in some interesting finds, particularly in North America.*

Once again, we set great store by the principle of actualism that we introduced in the first volume in this series, and accordingly we shall use the present as a key to a better understanding of our past. In the African plains many species of herbivore live together in herds: zebras and antelopes of various types graze together in a single group with sentinels that can alert all the animals to the presence of a predator, so that they can flee together en masse. To see why this works, imagine entering a bakery and having to choose a dessert. It's difficult, right? But we all know what to do; you think for a few minutes, choose, and pay. Now imagine that all the desserts in the bakery suddenly rise up and start whirling around you. How would you choose? The principle of mass flight functions in the same way, providing the predator with too many moving targets and confusing it to such an extent that while it is still choosing, the potential prey escapes out of reach. Presumably *Dryosauruses* sought to act the same way, surviving the ferocious predators of the time by living together with other herbivorous dinosaurs ✳19 and making sudden and rapid sprints to get out of harm's way. In fact, in our story these small dinosaurs live in close association with sauropods in order to gain the protection offered by the herd of gigantic herbivores.

We recently mentioned an animal that was more developed in terms of mastication: *Camptosaurus* **20** ("bent lizard"). It was an ornithischian herbivore of considerable size, though still a midget compared to the enormous sauropods, and adults of the species could be more than nineteen feet long. Observing its skeleton and the many reconstructions that have been assembled—since *Camptosaurus* remains are among the most commonly discovered in the Morrison—it gives the impression of being a primitive relative of an *Iguanodon* or of the wonderful hadrosaurs that would enliven the landscapes of the Cretaceous period (and that we will get to know in the books to follow). In reality this innocuous-looking dinosaur conceals incredible evolutionary advances. Do you remember? We spoke about "rough" chewing by dryosaurs, but here we have the beginning of a true technological revolution: teeth, entrusted with the task of grinding food, positioned well back in the jaws, and probably

almost seems like something out of science fiction, simply indicates that the animal's jaw is hinged in such a way that it can rotate outward when the mandible rises. In this way the teeth can properly grind plants. The result is chewing—different from that of mammals, which move the mandible horizontally, but still very effective. The champions of this technological innovation were the hadrosaurs of the Cretaceous, but for the period *Camptosaurus* did quite well, and apparently was quite successful, given its wide distribution.

Camptosaurus is a relative of the more famous *Iguanodon*, but it has a different, broader forefoot, probably because of its different habits, and an even more marked tendency to walk on four legs. (Like its relative *Dryosaurus*, *Camptosaurus* could choose to move about on two or four legs.)

Ornithopods undoubtedly flourished, and their presence in the Morrison was only the prelude to the evolutionary symphony of forms that would

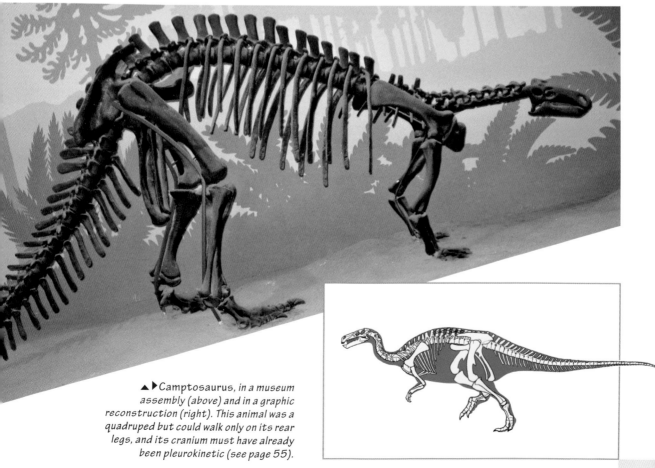

▲▶Camptosaurus, *in a museum assembly (above) and in a graphic reconstruction (right). This animal was a quadruped but could walk only on its rear legs, and its cranium must have already been pleurokinetic (see page 55).*

emerge in the Cretaceous. While not the only ornithischian dinosaurs to inhabit this territory of giants, they were definitely the most inoffensive.

Let's make the acquaintance of the Thyreophora, a sonorous name that means "shield bearers." The most famous thyreophore appears in the Morrison, and in our story: *Stegosaurus* ✱21. The name of this curious dinosaur means "plated reptile," and you can guess the reason at a single glance. The vaguely rhomboid-shaped bony plates that cover this animal's spine are certainly odd, and more than one paleontologist has beaten his head—for the most part metaphorically!—against the wall of these bony "tiles" and the mystery they pose.

Stegosaurus is an exceptional animal from any vantage point. It is an herbivore with relatively small teeth, not specialized like those of ornithopods. A quadruped, *Stegosaurus* probably could not move at even average speed, given its massive body, relatively short limbs, and extremely strange posture, with the rear portion of the spine pointed upward and terminating in a tall tail held parallel to the ground. Looking at its tail, however, we can immediately understand why our *Stegosaurus* is not concerned with speed. In fact, its tail, like that of all known stegosaurids, ends in a robust point armed with four very long, bony spines ✱22, a bit like the "morning star," a medieval club designed to poke a hole through the breastplate of a knight's armor. It is not difficult to imagine

▲ Heterodontosaurus. *Note the teeth that poke out from the open mouth. This animal was equipped with three types of teeth, very similar to the typical dentition of mammals such as human beings: pre-canines (similar to incisors), canines, and post-canines (similar to molars).*

✱21
page 24
panel 2

that a single blow from this armed tail, even an indirect one, could cause horrifying wounds. It was clearly an excellent defensive system.

However, paleontologists have long speculated about the characteristic that gives *Stegosaurus* its name: its "plates" **✳23**. Today we still do not know the precise function of these structures, and paleontologists do not even agree about how these plates were arranged on the animal, or the angle at which they "sprouted" from the body. Many different functions for the plates have been hypothesized: that they might have been used to signal recognition, or as solar panels, or as shields for defending the animal's sides. There is still no definitive answer; however, recent studies suggest that one function of the plates was as a sort of "identity card" to distinguish individual animals.

Like all well-known dinosaurs, *Stegosaurus* also plays a role in the myths about the dinosaurs' disappearance. Its arched back and the width of its pelvis have led some to hypothesize the presence of a "second brain." In fact the *Stegosaurus*'s skull is quite small, and for this reason some twentieth-century scientists had proposed the presence of an enormously enlarged nerve center on the spine, near the pelvis, which might have controlled much of the animal's movements and compensated for its extremely small principal brain. This theory has still not been proven, but it has met with notable success in nonscientific circles and has contributed to the perpetration of the idea of dinosaurs as slow, stupid animals. (If only this could be explained to an enraged *Stegosaurus* on the attack!) Yet all dinosaurs had an enlarged spinal medulla or ganglion in the pelvis; it was just not as large, proportionally, as that found in *Stegosaurus*.

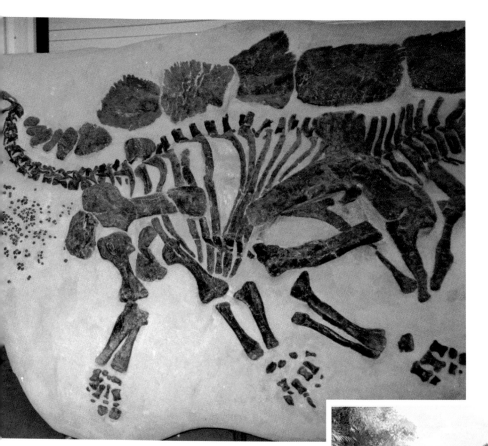

◀ Stegosaurus, one of the most famous dinosaurs in the world. This large plated herbivore had a rather small cranium but was heavily armed; according to some scholars, we cannot be completely certain about even the arrangement of the plates on its body, as seen in this example.

▲ A Stegosaurus skeleton just as it was discovered, almost perfectly connected anatomically. It is possible to make out the armor of the throat (scattered beneath the neck) and to see that the dorsal plates are not mplanted in the skeleton, but are separate, indicating that they were "mounted" in the animal's skin and not directly attached to the bones—making the task of reconstruction somewhat more difficult.

✳23
page 24
panel 4

▼ A reconstruction of Stegosaurus in an illustration from 1897. Note that the animal has been depicted in a very "reptilian" manner, with an armature of scales, almost like a crocodile's, covering its sides. (www.search4 dinosaurs.com)

The Jurassic in the Rest of the World

The picture that emerges from the fossil finds of the Morrison is not absolutely unique. While there are some cases of specific fossil fauna that do not have equivalents in other parts of the world—for example, Cretaceous-era fauna in China, in what is called the "Jehol biota"—the Late Jurassic is rather constant throughout the world in terms of animals. All over the planet, there are gigantic sauropods and mighty theropods that can be dated to the Jurassic. For example, the area of Tendaguru, in Africa, has yielded fossil remains of enormous animals, including the first *Brachiosaurus* known to man, and the fauna composition of this deposit is extraordinarily similar to that of the Morrison. Indeed, there are sauropods very similar to *Barosaurus*, *Brachiosaurus*, and *Dicraeosaurus*, which represent a group of sauropods that are unknown in the northern continents; stegosaurs such as *Kentrosaurus*; small ornithischians such as *Dryosaurus*; and the large carnivores *Allosaurus* and *Ceratosaurus*, as well as *Elaphrosaurus*, which is typical of this African region.

Camptosaurus, the ornithopod we have gotten to know in our story, also appears in Europe, as seen in Spain, where an *Allosaurus* has been discovered that is completely similar to those found in North America. It is probably even the same species as those in the Morrison. There are also fragmentary *Stegosaurus* remains in Europe, along with the *Dacentrurus* genus from the Jurassic in England. Chinese fauna are extremely similar as well, including enormous sauropods such as *Mamenchisaurus*, which has one of the longest necks in the history of life on earth; large allosaurids such as

▲ Skeleton of Tuojiangosaurus, a Chinese stegosaurid, exhibited in the dinosaur gallery of the Natural History Museum in London. The structure of the body is typical of Stegosauruses, but the spinal plates are narrower and sharper.

Yangchuanosaurus; and stegosaurids such as *Tuojiangosaurus*.

These "constant" fauna may have various implications, but one conclusion that seems valid is that dinosaurs at the end of the Jurassic had attained a sort of perfection for the environments of that moment, and therefore their forms became consistent more or less everywhere, since comparable environments recurred all over the planet. At the beginning of the Cretaceous, fauna remained quite similar to that of the late Jurassic, although there were new attempts to threaten the predominance of the Jurassic giants.

✳ *Volume 4*
Growing Up in the Cretaceous
Scipionyx

GLOSSARY

Aeolian: formed by the wind.

Air sacs: structures that form part of a bird's breathing apparatus and are located more or less throughout the animal's body, even in its bones.

Alimentary regime: an animal's diet, that is, what it normally eats.

Characteristic: an element of an organism, usually anatomical, that can be described and given a value in analyzing the category of organisms it belongs to.

Clade: a taxonomic grouping of all the descendants of a common ancestor.

Ectotherm: literally, an organism that bases its body temperature on that of the external environment. Today it is a term that is becoming obsolete.

Fluvial: formed by rivers.

Food processing: the action of preparing food for digestion, as by mastication.

Homeothermy: the ability of an organism to maintain a constant body temperature.

Home range: the territory where an organism normally carries out its activities.

International Code of Zoological Nomenclature (ICZN): a series of rules established by an international commission and followed whenever scientists name a newly discovered organism.

Metabolism: the totality of chemical and physical reactions that occur in a living being.

Pleurokinetic hinge: the moving dental and jaw joints that work together to form a primitive mastication system adopted by many ornithischians.

Postmortem: "after death." Indicates any moment after an organism expires; it is a term usually employed in taphonomy.

Super-predator: a predator at the top of a "food pyramid." In practical terms, this is a predator that no other animals hunt.

Acknowledgments

For their help and support both direct and indirect, Matteo Bacchin would like to thank (in no particular order) Marco Signore; Luis V. Rey; Eric Buffetaut; Silvio Renesto; Sante Bagnoli; Joshua Volpara; his dear friends Mac, Stefano, Michea, Pierre, and Santino; and everybody at Jurassic Park Italia. But he thanks above all his mother, his father, and Greta, for the unconditional love, support, and feedback that have allowed him to realize this dream.

Marco Signore would like to thank his parents, his family, Marilena, Enrico di Torino, Sara, his Chosen Ones (Claudio, Rino, and Vincenzo), la Compagnia della Rosa e della Spada, Luis V. Rey, and everybody who has believed in him.

For the photographs provided in the essay section, special thanks to: Fabio Manucci, Giacinto De Vivo, Domenico Difraia, Alessio Capobianco, and David Goldman (www.search4dinosaurs.com).

DINOSAURS

1 THE JOURNEY: *Plateosaurus*

We follow the path of a great herd of *Plateosaurus* from the sea—populated by ichthyosaurs—through the desert and mountains, to their nesting places. Their trek takes place beneath skies plied by the pterosaur *Eudimorphodon*, and under the watchful eye of the predator *Liliensternus*.

We discover what life was like on our planet during the Triassic period, and how the dinosaurs evolved.

(In bookstores now)

2 A JURASSIC MYSTERY: *Archaeopteryx*

What killed the colorfully plumed *Archaeopteryx*? Against the backdrop of a great tropical storm, we search for the perpetrator among the animals that populate a Jurassic lagoon, such as the small carnivore *Juravenator*, the pterosaur *Pterodactylus*, crocodiles, and prehistoric fish.

We discover how dinosaurs spread throughout the world in the Jurassic period and learned to fly, and how a paleontologist interprets fossils.

(In bookstores now)

3 THE HUNTING PACK: *Allosaurus*

We see how life unfolds in a herd of *Allosaurus* led by an enormous and ancient male, as they hunt *Camarasaurus* and the armored *Stegosaurus* in groups, look after their young, and struggle amongst themselves. A young and powerful *Allosaurus* forces its way into the old leader's harem. How will the confrontation end?

We discover one of the most spectacular ecosystems in the history of the Earth: the Morrison Formation in North America.

(In bookstores now)